Cornu

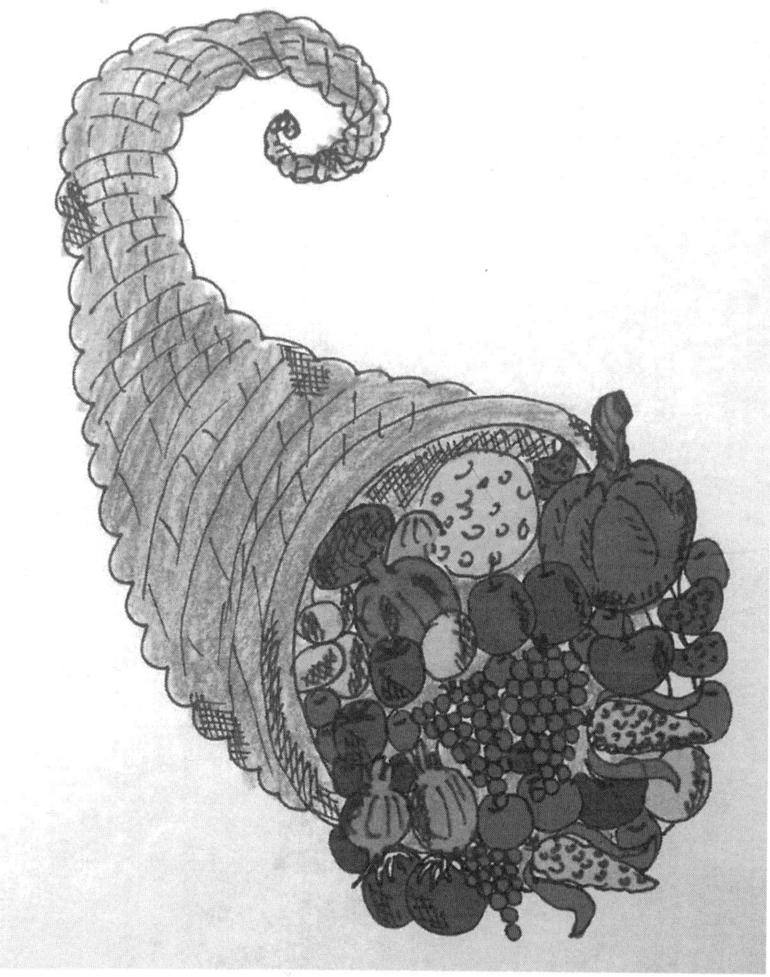

**Poetry, fiction and articles by Hammersmith Young Writers.
Cover art by Tyler O'Shea.**

Cornucopia

Published by Sheep Anthologies

Website: https://sheepanthologies.wordpress.com/

Contact: batterseayoungwriters@hotmail.com

ISBN: 978-1-326-63840-5

Copyright © 2016

All rights reserved. Works are published with permission from their respective author or artist. This anthology is a work of fiction. Names, characters, places and incidents are a product of the author's imagination, or if real, are used fictitiously. All work is assumed to have been produced by the stated author, original and free of copyright. The publisher accepts no responsibility for any infringement on behalf of the author, whether intentional or otherwise.

CONTENTS

Front Cover art: *'Cornucopia'* by Tyler O'Shea

Page	Author
6	Editor's Note

8	**Year 7: Fiction – Stories reflecting transition**
9	Afomeya Gultte
12	Ainhoa Reyes
17	Ariel Di Pompo
21	Bonnie Parkinson
23	Catarina Ferreira Xavier
25	Daisy Mann
28	Giorgia Abdel Nour
29	Kizzy Bonsu
33	Laureen Cabungcal
37	Magdalene Fre
40	Maya Gizachew
44	Maya Hafez
49	Sandy Saber

51	**Year 8: Poetry – Acrostic**
52	Annabelle Hogan
53	Bethel Tezera
54	Caitlin Oliver
55	Charis Ekanayaka
57	Delina Aron
58	Rebecca Thomas

CONTENTS

Front Cover art: *'Cornucopia'* by Tyler O'Shea

Page	Author
59	**Year 8: Poetry – Cinquain**
60	Annabelle Hogan
61	Bethel Tezera
62	Caitlin Oliver
63	Charis Ekanayaka
64	Jessica Garcia

Page	Author
65	**Year 8: Poetry – Clerihew**
66	Bethel Tezera
67	Charis Ekanayaka
68	Jade Genniges
69	Jessica Garcia
70	Rebecca Thomas

Page	Author
71	**Year 8: Poetry – Diamanté**
72	Annabelle Hogan
73	Annabelle Hogan and Bethel Tezera

Page	Author
74	**Year 8: Poetry - Etheree**
75	Bethel Tezera
76	Charis Ekanayaka
77	Jade Genniges
78	Jessica Garcia
79	Rebecca Thomas

CONTENTS

Front Cover art: *'Cornucopia'* by Tyler O'Shea

Page	Author
80	Year 9: Articles – Using writing prompts from the Metro
81	Year 9: Articles – Slang and Puns
82	Delia Rainone and Nicole Hidat

Page	Author
83	Year 9: Articles – sexism and stereotypes
84	Delia Rainone
85	Hyabel Kidane
86	Shauna Magee-Foster

Page	Author
87	Year 9: Articles – Fast food and culture
88	Hyabel Kidane and Nicole Hidat
89	Shauna Magee-Foster

Page	Author
90	Year 9: Articles – Interpreting newspaper headlines
91	Delia Rainone
92	Hyabel Kidane
93	Shauna Magee-Foster

Editor's Note

Welcome to **Cornucopia**, the 5th creative writing collection from *Sheep Anthologies*.

Sheep Anthologies is a publishing enterprise for young people between the ages of 11 to 19 in secondary education. It aims to inspire students to develop a lifelong passion for creative writing through participation in a 6 week project with an opportunity for publication. The project was developed in 2011 under the Every Child Matters Framework, focusing on 5 key principles from the Children's Act 2004. As **Cornucopia** is a creative collection (and we all know that policies can be rather dull!) let's do this through verse. An *acrostic* is much more fun:

Sheep (Anthologies)

Stay safe
Health first
Enjoy and achieve
Economic wellbeing
Positive contribution

Over 5 years, *Sheep Anthologies* has produced 5 collections: **Passion** (2011), **Transition** (2012), **Kaleidoscope** (2013), **The Great Big Book of Stories** (2014) and now **Cornucopia** (2016), helping students to enjoy and achieve and to make a positive contribution in their community.

It is therefore with great pleasure that I present to you our 2016 anthology, **Cornucopia**, containing fiction by Year 7, poetry by Year 8, newspaper articles by Year 9 and artwork by Year 10. I would like to thank the students who worked immensely hard and showed great dedication to improving their writing.

I hope you enjoy their work!

Leilanie

Year 7: Stories to reflect transition
- Into secondary school
- Through life's events

Year 7: Fiction
Afomeya Gultte

THE MYSTERY OF YEAR 7

Hi, my name is Aaliyahma, but people call me Yafo. Today you're going to be reading about my story.

Yesterday, I got word of my new school. I was accepted to all, but I chose Mayballeen Girls' school in Hammersmith. The school I'm in is Lorryelle school in Fulham. My primary school is wonderful; the education is good, the teachers are delightful and the most important reason why I love the school is that I feel safe.

Today is my last day of primary school, so I'm saying goodbye to all my friends. I hope I will still meet up with them someday.

Two months later!!!

✌✌✌

Today is a new day, a new start and a new year. It's the first day at Mayballeen. I walk into school scared, not knowing the way around and petrified of meeting new people. However, I feel very confident and secure after meeting my form tutor, Miss Elizalde. After finding Ellie and Angelika, my close friends from primary school, I feel the flutter of butterflies in my belly, as I can't wait to make new friends. I'm starting to, after talking with many people.

👍👍👍

Later on that week…

👍👍👍

I'm in the same form as Kaya, in the same set as Alina and Hanna, and I've been introduced to new friends Esme, Khamera and Casia. I understand that it is hard sometimes to like everybody, but it's much better than having enemies. Sometimes though, making a bridge with somebody you just met can be hard.

Days fly by rapidly and I begin to discover the labyrinths of corridors and learn new subjects that I didn't learn in primary school, like French and Design Technology. During my time in the school, I've gained more independence and confidence. I'm also *way* more busy with all the homework. There are other differences between primary and secondary school. One disadvantage of primary school is that you stay in the same class, but in secondary school, you change classrooms for every lesson, which I like. And at lunchtime in primary school you have to be outside, even if it's raining. Homework is different too. Primary school practised spelling, while in secondary school, we write essays.

But there are advantages of primary school too. On the last day, you watch films, play games, but in secondary school, you don't. I know…so unfair!

My tutor will be the same for the entire year in Year 7. Don't tell anybody, but if you get Miss Elizalde, you are a lucky student. You'll stay on her good side as she is the friendliest teacher and the most passionate.

I hope you enjoyed my story about my transition into Year 7. There are going to be more stories, like my transition into Year 8 and about my GCSEs. So, goodbye for now, and I hope to tell you another story, soon.

Year 7: Fiction
Ainhoa Reyes

ODD ONE OUT – HOME SCHOOL TO SECONDARY

Today is the day. Today is the day I go back to school after 5 years of being tutored by my mother. Today is the day I go back to school after the *'accident.'* My father died when I was only 7. His death made me want to be home-schooled; and I have been, but mother said that I should not dwell on the past. Words can't describe the fear I am feeling, but my thumping heart can. Today is the day I move on.

"Noa…Noa…NOA EDEN, YOU ARE GOING TO BE LATE FOR SCHOOL," Mother exclaims enthusiastically.

And that's my cue.

👍👍👍

Slowly, I make my way through the green gate and I suddenly see hundreds of recognisable faces. My neighbour,

Lola, is attending St. Helena as well, so we decided to meet in the canteen before registration. The problem is, I do not have a clue where it is.

"Hey, I'm Casey. I was wondering if you know where the cafeteria is?" A voice says behind me.

I turn around and see a girl who looks like me. She has a black blazer, a chequered tie and a long skirt that reaches her knees. On the other hand, her hair is blonde instead of brown and she has green eyes, not blue.

"I don't, but you can come with me as I'm looking for it too," I answer.

"That would be wonderful. What is your name?"

"My name is Noa. Now, let's go and find the canteen."

👍👍👍

"Good morning Year 7. My name is Mr. Robinson and I will be your P.E. teacher."

"Good morning Mr. Robinson," we all sing in unison.

"I have an idea what the majority of you are feeling. Fear? Worry? Stress? But, you have to remember that it is the first day for all of you, and you are now going to be a family for at least 5 years."

All at once, my heart beat slows down. My body relaxes. My breath decelerates. All at once, I realise that everyone else is experiencing what I am.

"Now, go and get changed and then we will start with the warm ups," Mr. Robinson says.

I make my way to the changing room with the other students. Socks are being thrown through the air and conversations consume the room. I put on my P.E. shirt and I take off my skirt. All at once, the socks are static and the conversations have come to a conclusion. My eyes dart around the room and I notice something; everyone is looking at me. My brain flicks through all the possibilities of why I became the centre of attention. Something clicks into place and I realise why. I feel my cheeks become crimson and the never-ending silence become deafening in my head. My eyes permit the river to flood from them and my body becomes weak. My father was not all I lost in the 'accident'; I lost my right leg, (which was replaced by an artificial limb). Unexpectedly, hugs and words of affection caress me.

"Don't worry, Noa."

"Do not cry; it is nothing to be ashamed about."

"Noa, we love you, no matter what you look like."

Through the blur of my tears, I see Casey's silhouette. She looks into my eyes and says, **"Be proud of who you are, and not ashamed of how someone else sees you."**

I guess secondary is not so bad after all.

※ ※ ※

"How was school, Noa?" Mother asks, while I enter the house.

"It was…surprising," I manage to say.

"What do you mean?" Mother responds, with a crease forming on her forehead.

"Well, if you think that perfect is possible, then that is what today was."

👍👍👍

    A lot has changed; for example, the fact that for P.E. I have a gym, not a garden. Or that there are thirty people in a room, not just two. Or even the fact that I have to repeat my name a million times in a day. But what has not changed is me. I am still the girl that does not have a father. I am still the girl with a prosthetic leg. I am still Noa Eden and nothing will be able to change that. I might be becoming more independent and I might be becoming more mature, but nothing will be able to change my past and I am okay with that. I should have realised sooner that school is not as scary as it sounds. You make new friendships that will hopefully last forever.

Year 7: Fiction
Ariel Di Pompo

THE FIRST DAY OF YEAR 7

Amanda walked through the dark, painted gates of her new secondary school. This was the start of something new; new people, new teachers and even new subjects. Nobody else from her primary school had been accepted into her new school, so she was determined to make friends. She tried to imagine what her classmates would be like. Would they have the same interests as her, or would they be rude and snobby?

Amanda looked down at the map to her form room, 7HS. As she stepped towards it, her heart raced. She hoped she wasn't late; she had to make a good first impression. She didn't want to feel awkward turning up late.

Steadily opening the door, she heard loud laughs and whispering. Glad it wasn't at her, she went in and propped herself onto a chair with her name written on it. Her bag seemed extremely heavy. *How can I possibly carry this every day,* she wondered. She set it down beside her chair.

Suddenly, she noticed that everyone had become quiet. Their new teacher, Ms Thornten, strided in. "Good morning, 7HS!" she shouted.

"Good morning, Ms Thornten," they exclaimed back.

Ms Thornten was quite a scary-looking woman, which made everyone quiet for a while. Amanda looked around her neat classroom as Ms Thornten called out the register. A few of her classmates smiled at her, which sent butterflies to her tummy. *Maybe I don't have to worry too much, after all,* she thought. Soon after her welcome assembly about new school life in Year 7, she was given a timetable of what classes to go to for lessons. First, it was art; her favourite subject. While she was heading to the art department, she realised lots of people must like art, just like her, and this could be a way to make new friends.

When she arrived to her art class, she was impressed with the art that was hanging up; like the oil pastelled rainbow and the paintings of animals. This is where she always wanted to be; this had brought back memories of her primary school.

In her lesson, they had to draw cups and a jug. Amanda was excited and so was the girl sitting next to her, called Skylar. The girls exchanged smiles; they both seemed to have a lot in common.

Amanda looked at Skylar's paper. It was amazing. "You're really good at art," Amanda said.

"You really think so? I prefer yours," Skylar replied, gushing.

Amanda and Skylar talked throughout the lesson as they painted. Then Skylar asked if Amanda wanted to hang out at break and lunch. Amanda squealed in delight, "Yes, that would be fun!"

I'm finally making a friend, she thought. Amanda couldn't focus in her next lesson and looked forward to break for that hour. Finishing her Maths work, she ran at break time to look for Skylar. Skylar sat on the table waiting for Amanda with a warm smile. She sat down and was about to chat, when some sixth formers started laughing at them.

"They're so tiny!" the sixth formers smirked.

Skylar jumped to her feet. "And I thought you lot were supposed to be role models!" Skylar screamed.

Skylar sat down again as the sixth formers muttered and walked away, their smiles fading.

Amanda stared at Skylar whilst giggling. "How could you possibly do that?"

"I stand for what's true," Skylar answered calmly.

Amanda admired Skylar a lot. She decided that this was her first best friend in Year 7.

Year 7: Fiction
Bonnie Parkinson

BELLA'S NEW LIFE

It was a sunny September day. Bella awoke to birds singing; there was a feeling of mixed emotions, sending butterflies to her tummy. This was unusual for Bella's personality. She was usually super confident and extremely outgoing. Bella stared in the mirror, despising the itchy, dull uniform. She took a deep breath, reached for her rucksack and set off for her first day at Francis High School.

When Bella arrived at school, she was assigned to form 7F. As she walked into her new form room, she hurried to see if her best friend was in yet. She jumped and gave her best friend a hug. Her best friend's name was Sophie and even though they were best friends, they both had different personalities. Bella was extremely eager to make new friends and couldn't wait to get started with the 'friendship exercises'.

Bella felt torn. She wanted to make new friends, but didn't want to hurt Sophie's feelings, as Sophie was less eager to socialise with new people. However, Bella decided to put her fears aside and embrace all of the opportunities of her new high school. She could seek new friends, while also trying to remain loyal to Sophie and her old primary school friends. Bella knew that making new friendships didn't mean that she would have to end her old friendships.

👍 👍 👍

Some weeks had now passed and Bella had experienced many ups and downs, but she was relieved that her fears from her first day had drifted away not long after she had started school. Forming new friends had been very exciting and interesting for Bella.

👍 👍 👍

After the first term of high school, Sophie made new friends who had the same interests as her, as well as her quieter personality. Sophie spent her time between her new friends; Janet, Chloe and Emma, and also with Bella. So, even though she made new friends, she never forgot Bella.

Year 7: Fiction
Catarina Ferreira Xavier

THE BETRAYAL

When you move into Year 7, you might not know anyone and need to make new friends. But are they always faithful to you? Or, are they just using you?

At Annabel's first day at her new school, Cahland Secondary School, she made a new best friend called Meghan. They did everything together. But one day, Meghan and Annabel were having a big argument. They were very angry at each other and got mean to each other. Ever since then, they started to drift apart and both went in different directions. Annabel was lonely and confused. She had to find some more friends.

She was shy about this at first, but she knew she had to overcome her fear of talking to other people. Then, she met three girls: Lizzy, Mia and Francesca and they became the best of friends. Life was getting better again.

Annabel learned that settling into secondary school isn't easy, because not everyone is what they seem. Then again, she found the best friends that she could ever find. She just needed to be a bit more open.

Year 7: Fiction
Daisy Mann

THE NEW CLASS AT WORLD ACADEMY

Hey there! I'm Alfred F. Jones, and I'm in the new Year 7 class of 'World Academy'. I'll explain; World Academy is a secondary school in London and it invites one student from each country around the world to join Year 7, and go up to sixth form. Of course, I represent the heroic USA! My friend Arthur represents Britain; he's the only person I'll know going into this new school year, which is a bit unfortunate, but we'll meet lots of new people.

I remember my mum wanting to drop me to school on my first day, but I wanted to show her how independent I was, so I took the bus. Besides, Arthur was on the bus and that way, because I was really nervous, we were able to go into school together. There were some other kids on the bus wearing our uniform, which was a blue blazer and shirt, with black, formal trousers for the boys and a red, pleated skirt and white blouse for the girls. We met someone representing France; funnily enough his name was Francis.

I'm pretty sure school started at 8.30A.M, although we were early by 10 minutes, so Arthur and I went to Starbucks. I remember Arthur saying something about 'Tea is better than coffee, you silly American', but it was okay because the lady at the cash register said I looked very smart.

When I first got to the school, I couldn't believe what I was seeing. There was a large archway to walk through and there were a lot of students walking through there. I was getting really nervous because I wanted to make a good first impression, of course. There were also a few older pupils waiting for us, to tell us where to go, which was super helpful.

Our first lesson was Science, and I really love Science. We had to find our way to the Science classroom, which was really hard to do, but I asked a girl in Year 9 to help me and she did. I felt a bit embarrassed coming in to the lesson late. My teacher said it was okay because we were new.

At break I was very excited to see all the food they had. I heard from my brother Matthew that the food was better than

Primary school. I managed to find Arthur too; he was talking to some people he must have met in his lesson. I think one, Antonio, was representing Spain and the other, Gilbert, was representing Germany or Austria. I walked up to say 'hi' and Arthur introduced me to them; they were really kind and came to eat with us.

The rest of the day went fairly fast and by the end, I really wanted to stay at school. But I went home with our two new friends and Arthur.

Being in Year 7 is so awesome! I'm way more independent and I feel a lot more responsible for my own life now. I can't wait until Year 8!

Year 7: Fiction
Giorgia Abdel Nour

THE BIG MISTAKE

Once upon a time, there were two girls called Aria and Daisy. They had been friends for three years. But one day, the girls had a fight. They said mean things to each other and called each other names. They didn't hang around together for a while.

At school, Aria started to smile across the room to Daisy, and Daisy would do it back to Aria. After a few months, they tried to get along by confessing the truth to each other that they still wanted to be friends. They shared ideas that both of them liked, like going to gymnastics together. Aria started to compliment Daisy. And Daisy said nice things back.

The girls began to play in the park together. Bit by bit, they learned from their big mistake – that it wasn't good to lie and fight.

And they lived happily ever after.

Year 7: Fiction
Kizzy Bonsu

GROWING BRANCHES

Tentatively, I walked towards the dorm rooms. With my bags in hand, I walked into my bedroom to see another five girls laying on their beds. There was a minute of awkward silence. I took my suitcase and walked across the huge, brightly-lit room. Once I'd finished unpacking, I glanced around the room.

I heard a knock at the door; it creaked open. A tall, thin lady appeared wearing a tight brown bun. She eyed the five girls and they left the room immediately. I stepped back, accidently knocking over a small, black box. I picked it up and put it in my rucksack. The tall lady was distracted by the guards, so I quickly brushed past her. I ran into the hall. A large number of girls, including my dorm-mates glanced and stared. I froze on the spot, open-mouthed.

"It must be you," said the tall, thin lady.

"Who, me?" I said.

"Yes, you. You know what you have done," she said.

I was confused. "Sorry? I don't know what you mean."

The tall, thin lady glared at my five dorm-mates and me. "Detention for all six of you after school."

Detention on my first day? I just wished things would finally go my way…

👎👎👎

After I composed myself, I left the hall. I knew I couldn't go back to the dorm with the mysterious lady lurking around there. I dashed to the storage cupboard. Then I remembered the black box I picked up earlier. That must have been what the tall lady had been angry about. I pulled it out of my rucksack and opened it. Inside was a heart-shaped twig. I popped it back in my bag and sat down to think. Did the box belong to the lady? I would return it to her during detention and apologise. I hadn't meant to steal it; I had just picked it up. What seemed like minutes was actually several hours. I gasped; it was the end of the first day. Detention!

Slowly, I opened the door and scuttled across the corridor. Detention went quickly. It was actually easier than I thought it would be. We had to write lines. While we were writing, I quietly placed the black box back under the tall lady's desk. My five dorm-mates saw this and smiled.

👍👍👍

Dawn broke. I was wide awake. Anyway, it would give me loads of time to get ready for my lessons and to think. I still didn't know the secret of the mysterious heart-shaped twig in the box.

First period was rowing. We all grabbed our gear and went towards the water. The rest of the class was waiting. Their impatient faces and rapid foot-tapping made me uncomfortable. After 5 minutes of preparation, we finally got in the water. As soon as we sat down in the boat, something felt wrong. The current was way too strong.

I kept silent as we went on. I was with my five dorm-mates; they all seemed much more open and calm. We moved swiftly across the water until we hit something hard. I fell out of the boat. The murky, green water wrapped me up like a tightly-closed parcel.

Suddenly I felt something clasp my arm. It was a hand. It dragged me slowly up. Everything after that became a blur.

☞ ☞ ☞

I woke up in my bed. Five heads popped up in front of me. I blinked twice. It was my dorm-mates. I slowly sat up and smiled.

"Thanks for putting the box under Miss Dragneel's desk," said one of them.

"Yeah, we didn't steal it. We found it, but we didn't know it was hers," said another.

We all looked at each other and broke into laughter. We talked and talked for ages. I actually really enjoyed myself. I guess it wasn't that bad having some new friends, especially now I'm in boarding school. I remembered Miss Dragneel's box. My five new friends were like the heart-shaped twig. It's just like growing new branches.

Year 7: Fiction
Laureen Cabungcal

THE BEAM OF LIGHT

Olivia Smith rose from her bed not realising her alarm was still on. BEEP, BEEP, BEEP!

She tied her brunette hair up into a high ponytail and stood up. With her arms stretched wide, she yawned and grudgingly went downstairs. It was on this fine morning that Olivia would start her new path going to secondary school…

"I don't really want to go to secondary school, mum…" she quietly announced, as she was the only pupil from her primary school to go to her new school. She was nervous. Scared. Afraid. Not knowing anybody and the thought of not having anyone to talk to… However, a couple of minutes after a talk between Olivia and her mother, her mother insisted she go. So, she unwillingly dragged herself up the stairs to put on her secondary school uniform.

The uniform was simple; a plain blue blazer, a navy jumper, a light blue shirt, tights, a chequered skirt (with the colours black and blue) and her smart, black shoes. Olivia soon got dressed and was ready with her backpack, standing by the door. Her mother smiled gently at her, giving Olivia comfort and warmth inside her for the day ahead.

☞ ☞ ☞

Olivia and her mother travelled around twenty-five minutes by car and soon arrived at the school. She had butterflies in her stomach throughout the journey. There was no turning back. Olivia's mum waved her a big goodbye and hugged her. Olivia wondered if her mother could feel her heartbeat thumping against her when they hugged. After her mother left, Olivia went through the school gates to start the first day of Year 7.

The secondary school was a private all-girls school. Olivia constantly thought of not having someone beside her, although she shrugged, knowing the beam of light at the end of this new path was still available. The school was very modern, with red bricks and spotless windows – not even a fingerprint!

As Olivia continued to walk to the place that others called a 'form room', she suddenly felt a gentle tap on her right shoulder.

"Hello!" said a girl's voice.

Olivia turned round to face the girl, but she was gone. Vanished! Disappeared! Olivia raised her eyebrows in such surprise; however, she then saw some movement behind the thick, oak tree. She giggled and ran towards the tree to find the girl hiding.

The girl was pale and had blue eyes, as deep as the big, blue ocean, blonde hair and thin lips. She looked at Olivia, smiled and remarked, "Charlotte. My name." Soon after, she ran away.

Olivia knew she had met someone who she could talk to. She had found a friend.

👍👍👍

Olivia went into her form room, shyly, but gasped with delight when she realised Charlotte sat at a desk, near the back of the room, by the window. Her friend was new to this school as well! She walked towards Charlotte as the teacher came into the room.

"Stand up, please," the teacher asked, while the pupils were still talking. In less than a minute, the children quietly stood up.

Charlotte gestured to Olivia to come to her. Olivia crept towards her. Charlotte handed her a small piece of paper. The note read: "Meet me at the oak tree at break!"

Olivia stuck her thumb up, giving her a smile and giggled quietly, making sure the stern teacher didn't hear. Charlotte smiled back.

It was then that Olivia felt the beam of light bright again, shining over her new path.

Year 7: Fiction
Magdalene Fre

TAKING YOU THROUGH MY WORLD: DIVERSION FROM SOCIETY

I'm an ordinary boy in an ordinary world, but one thing is dragging me away from society. My brother Andy has got… has got…

Cancer.

I'm going through a tough time. I feel as though my head is full of trapped questions. Tears keep on running down my face. I feel empty, useless and worthless.

My mother, Micheala, and my dad called Aaron are suffering too. It hurts so much to see them cry. I need help, but I don't know who to talk to. I am only 12 and I feel like my world is falling apart. It's weird because me and my brother don't have much affection, but this is no game and I feel like this is the only time I get to be closer to him. My heart melts every moment I see him. I don't feel like waking up in the morning to find out my brother is in hospital; it breaks me apart every time.

I'm so upset. He has got pancreatic cancer; it's a terminal illness and I know they have no cure. Knowing that any day my brother might be gone is a life changing experience. I miss him already, and so much that I don't know what to do. A piece of my heart is missing.

I'm leaving right now to go to the hospital and I'm afraid. Oh, his face; it breaks my heart! He is losing weight and the chemotherapy has made him lose his hair. Questions keep on bubbling in my head and I can't seem to pop the answers.

We are getting the results tomorrow to see if the tumour is still there. See you soon!

👍👍👍

Although my brother has got cancer, you always have to remember that life is worth living for. I love my brother and hope he knows that without him, my world will be shattered into a million pieces. I feel numb with fear and all my thoughts are frozen in time. I feel so blue, and at times ask myself: Why is this happening to me? It feels so strange.

But, at the end of the day, you have to move forward and I need to remember that he is in good hands. I will be with him every step of the way through this battle with cancer.

Remember, you who is reading this, if you ever get caught by things like this in life, remember to stay strong. And most of all, remember to be brave.

Year 7: Fiction
Maya Gizachew

LIFE AT BROOKLYN HIGH

On a bright Monday morning, the alarm clock went off in Katie's room at 06:30. Katie wondered why she had to wake up so early. She glanced around the room and saw something hanging on the door – her secondary school uniform. She jumped out of bed and went to take a shower.

Patiently, Katie's mum waited in the dining room with her favourite breakfast on a plate – chocolate chip pancakes! Katie was told she had to leave home to go and get Haylee, her bestie, and go to school with her at 07:30. As she ate her breakfast, Katie's thoughts were on Brooklyn High.

After breakfast, she rushed into her room, got changed and went to get Haylee, while Katie's mum got the car out of the garage. Full of excitement, Haylee and Katie talked nonstop about Year 7 and what it would be like. Katie was excited, happy and hopeful about making new friends and feeling at home. On the other hand though, Haylee admitted that she feared she would lose Katie. She also worried about all the work and not making friends. Katie reassured her that they would always be besties.

As they drew near school, Katie started talking about primary school and how much she would miss her friends. "But, I've been looking forward to this day for so long, and it's finally here," she exclaimed.

"I know," Haylee replied, "I'm really going to miss Year 6, but this could be a fresh start for us and we might even make new friends."

By request, Katie's mum dropped the girls at the end of the path leading towards their school, since they said they wanted to remember this day when they would leave 6 years later. Although they reached the end of the path, Katie and Haylee stopped in their tracks and their jaws dropped, quite low, in unison.

"Is this our new school?" Haylee murmured.

"You bet!" said Katie, excitedly.

As they walked through the gates, they were handed their timetables, a map of the school each and a list of all the teachers by some of the sixth formers. Luckily, Katie and Haylee were in the same form and at school for that day it was only Year 7s, so they got to spend the whole day with their form. The girls took part in a grand tour, got to meet their teachers, and got to know the other students in their form group. Since the teachers needed to plan tomorrow's lessons, the day finished at 13:30.

Haylee's mum came and picked the girls up from school and took them home. Katie and Haylee talked about school for 20 whole minutes. When they arrived back at Haylee's house, a plate of yummy snacks such as cookies and milk, cucumber and hummus and cereal bars had been laid out for them.

Later on, Katie's mum took Katie home for dinner and her mum heard all about the school. Funnily enough, Katie and Haylee were in different houses, but were saying the exact same things to their families over dinner; Katie found out an hour after dinner when she was sent to bed, as Haylee texted her. She'd been sent to bed too, to get ready for the next day.

Although she was tired, Katie was too excited for her next day and was so restless – but she dozed off anyway. Unfortunately for her parents, Katie got up at the crack of dawn, called up Haylee and asked her to come round for breakfast. Everyone was still sleeping in her house, but Katie didn't care; as long as she was together with Haylee.

Year 7: Fiction
Maya Hafez

OVERCOMING A FEAR

With acknowledgement to 'Fairy Tail' by Hiro Mashima

Overcoming a fear is an unpredictably hard action to perform. My fear isn't your usual 'fear'. It's a terror of making friends.

Meet me: Charlie Alex Clive, a typical teenage boy who is sheepish, disquieted and awkward. I don't seem to get along with others, most of the time, especially in my primary school. However, as my mother says, 'Everything will get better since you're going to high school!' I don't believe this, because as I mentioned, I am extremely antisocial and awkward; hard to get along with. Every time I speak to someone, whether boy or girl, I feel as if a shadow of anxiety is hanging onto my shoulder, pulling me down and the words don't exit my mouth. Many just laugh at me; I thought this would be my life forever. But before I knew it, EVERYTHING was going to change.

This is MY high school experience (so far)…

☞ ☞ ☞

It was around 7.45 as I boarded the congested train, about to start a different school. As the train was busy, I leaned against the silver pole, looking at the reflection of my onyx-coloured eyes, worried that their darkness made me seem moody. Soon enough, I was in Hammersmith, about to enter Thornton Secondary School, a mixed gender school. Many say it is strict, however, others say it is delightful. I was about to test these 'sayings' from MY point of view.

When I entered the school, people were socialising and I was the 'odd one out', sitting by myself. I felt like I didn't belong; as if I wasn't meant to be there. Suddenly, before I had time to notice, a thud vibrated the table. My eyes trudged upwards to see a girl happily smiling. She seemed friendly.

"Hello! Are you okay? You look lonely. I'm Arabella, by the way," she enunciates happily. Her aura was a rare one; extremely happy and upbeat.

I decided it was time to make friends. "I'm Charlie," I state, before smiling at her. Her smile widens. She looks extremely innocent, but, I feel as if she's going to be weird – in a good way, of course.

After a while, the teacher explained our courses and I was handed my timetable. Sadly, Arabella wasn't in my set, only my form. This made it harder for me; I felt lonelier than ever. Arabella had told me we'd still be the best of friends. When she said that, it had made me feel slightly better, however, I was still extremely sad.

Excluding that paragraph, my first lesson was Science. Great. Probably reproduction…

I exited my form room, entering Science class in classroom G8. The teacher, Mrs Goodall, led us to our tables. I sat with people who looked friendly. There was Mio, Ciel, Aaron, Gemma and Daniel. They seemed to get along, but I didn't feel like joining the conversation.

"Guys, you NEED to check out this anime called 'Fairy Tail'. It's awesome," Daniel said happily. The others all agreed to watch it. The name of this 'anime', Fairy Tail, intrigued me. I decided to search it on the Science computers. It looked extremely interesting, although the reviews were low.

After school finished, I went home and grabbed my Apple laptop. I began to watch the show and soon became addicted. It was about a girl, Lucy Heartfilia, a travelling Mage, who meets Natsu Dragneel. Natsu is a Mage looking for his foster parent, a Dragon named Igneel along with his best friend, Happy, a blue talking and flying cat. Shortly after they meet, Lucy is abducted to be sold as a slave by Bora of Prominence, who was posing as Salamander of Fairytail. Natsu rescues her and reveals that he is the real Salamander of Fairy Tail. He has the skills of a Dragon Slayer, a form of Lost Magic. He offers her membership into the Fairy Tail Guild, which she gladly accepts. Along with the armoured Mage, Erza Scarlet, Ice-Make Mage, Gray Fullbuster, and Happy, Lucy and Natsu become a team, performing various missions offered to the Fairy Tail Guild.

The next day at school, we had Science. My table began to speak about this anime and I decided to join in.

"Hey, I'm Charlie. I've watched Fairy Tail. It's extremely good," I exclaim joyfully. Their faces suddenly light up.

"That's great – let's be friends! I'm Mio. This is Ciel, Aaron, Gemma and Daniel," Mio said, while pointing at each individual.

We all begin to click and soon enough, we all became best friends. This was a sudden turn to MY story; nothing that I would have expected. My journey still carries on and I have the *bestest* of friends: Arabella, Daniel, Mio, Aaron, Ciel and Gemma.

I am Charlie Alex Clive and this is MY story.

Year 7: Fiction
Sandy Saber

CYBERBULLYING

In a new school, in a new year, there were two girls. One was called Marolina and the other was called Marian. They had been best friends since 2014.

But, one day, the girl called Marian said, "I don't want to be your BFF because you're too annoying."

So Marolina got upset, and Marian got mad.

After school, the girls went home and talked to their friends on Wattsapp. It started as chat, then Marian swore at Marolina and Marolina told Marian off.

Marolina showed the teacher a screenshot of the chat and both girls got in trouble. But, the problem wasn't solved. Yet.

Until… the girls said sorry to each other.

Now they are nice to each other and can forget about everything. Now they can start a new life in their new school.

Year 8: Poetry

Acrostic

The first letter of each line spells a word, usually the same word as in the title.

Year 8: Acrostic poetry
Annabelle Hogan

ANNABELLE

Always kind,

Never late.

Not rude

And a good friend.

Bacon lover.

Every day watches TV

Loves ice-cream

Loves fruit

Every day enjoys her sleep.

Year 8: Acrostic Poetry
Bethel Tezera

FEBRUARY: A FISHY START

Fish are so fishy.
Everyone loves fish and eggs,
Being a fish must be a dream,
Rowing through a lake filled with fish is my aspiration
U are crazy if you hate fish!
Almond-shaped fish are the best.
Respect fishes around the earth
You are fishy if you don't.

BETHEL: EGG LOVER

Between you and me...
Everyone should love eggs.
To me they taste delicious.
Have you ever tried them?
Eggs are *SO* tasty and smooth,
Lovely eggs are what I eat. What about you?

Year 8: Acrostic Poetry
Caitlin Oliver

BASKETBALL

Bounce the ball

And walk one step

Stop to shoot

Keep your eye on the net

Energy running through you

The time ticking

Bounce the ball

Again and again

Looking around; where are the team mates?

Long time to wait.

Year 8: Acrostic Poetry
Charis Ekanayaka

CHARIS

Cherishing life,

Hard working,

At home I always relax,

Relaxing is my reward,

Ice-cream with it too,

Shimmering ice-cream is amazing.

Year 8: Acrostic Poetry
Charis Ekanayaka

BASKETBALL

Basketball is my life

Amazing players inspire me

Shooting a hoop gives me delight

Ku-dunk is my favourite made-up basketball word

Exciting games get me really tense

Teams should practise every day;

"**B**all is life"

Always working as a community

Longing for the next game

Losing the game messes up my day!

Year 8: Acrostic Poetry
Delina Aron

DELINA ARON

Dinner is a winner

Every day you have options

Lots to pick from

I'd pick chocolate

Not too much though

And not too little

A favourite meal for me is chicken

Ready to eat at six

On Friday nights I eat with friends

Nandos is where it all begins…

Year 8: Acrostic Poetry
Rebecca Thomas

SPYAIR

Special to me and all your fans,

Personally, my favourite band of all time.

You lift me up when I'm down.

A pride and joy,

I love your music.

Rock out!

Year 8: Poetry

Cinquain

A short, usually unrhymed poem of 22 syllables distributed as 2,4,6,8,2 in 5 lines:

>Noun
>Description of noun
>Action
>Feeling or effect
>Synonym of the initial noun.

Year 8: Cinquain Poetry
Annabelle Hogan

AUTUMN

Autumn.

Lots of brown leaves

Trees swishing and swaying.

Cosy and warm all together

Harvest.

Year 8: Cinquain Poetry
Bethel Tezera

BALLET

Dancer
Is elegant
With a petit tu-tu
And some dancing, flexible shoes
Hyper.

LOTS OF BOOKS

Big books,
Dusty, big ones,
Reading, learning, thinking,
They are mysterious and good,
Have fun!

Year 8: Cinquain Poetry
Caitlin Oliver

RAINBOW

Rainbow

Bright, beautiful,

Lighting up the blue sky,

Makes people feel happy about themselves

Glowing.

Year 8: Cinquain Poetry
Charis Ekanayaka

BUNNY-HOP

Lively,
Always different,
Sweet, angelic bunnies,
Bunny-hopping kangaroo jumps,
Funny.

TOWNS

City.
Modern culture,
Business deals every day.
Lovely movement, mysterious,
Alive.

Year 8: Cinquain Poetry
Jessica Garcia

APPLES

Apples
Juicy and nice,
Worms want to go inside
But I make apple pie first
Yummy!

P.E.

P.E.
is good for you
running, dancing, skipping,
It's really good for your health too,
Netball.

Year 8: Poetry

Clerihew

A comic verse consisting of two couplets and a specific rhyming scheme: aabb.

Year 8: Clerihew Poetry
Bethel Tezera

TOASTIES

I like toast more than most
But loads of people boast
That my toast tastes delicious,
So then they get suspicious.

CREATIVITY

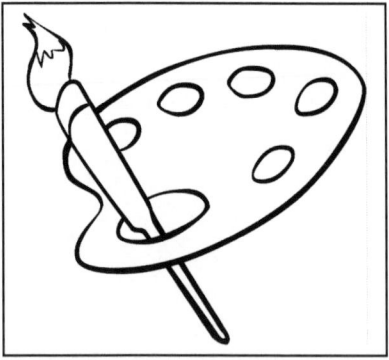

I find art fun,
While I draw out in the sun,
My paintings are alluring,
People find them reassuring.

Year 8: Clerihew Poetry
Charis Ekanayaka

LLAMAS

Llamas like to run around
While Alpacas manage to calm down
Llamas also jump on people
When they're standing like a steeple.

IPHONE

My iphone is my life,
People ask if it is my wife,
I'm on it twenty-four seven
Because I think it's heaven.

Year 8: Clerihew Poetry
Jade Genniges

CHRISTMAS DINNER

The doorbell rings

My oven dings

Delicious Christmas turkey roast,

Side dish of Xmas garlic toast.

MICROWAVE FOOD

When my microwave goes ding,

That can only mean one thing,

Ever since I've known you, food,

You've treated me well and never rude.

Year 8: Clerihew Poetry
Jessica Garcia

DOLPHINS

Dolphins are really nice,
I like them more than spicy rice
Good at jumping really high,
It looks to me like they can fly.

THE DOGS

The best pets are dogs
Sleeping as quietly as logs
And they run really fast
Looking like a fireball blast.

Year 8: Clerihew Poetry
Rebecca Thomas

MY CUTIE PIE

Alpaca, you gave me a shove
You really wore out my love
I wanted to take you home,
But you were too accident prone.

Year 8: Poetry

Diamante

A seven-lined contrast poem set up in a diamond shape:

A noun
Two adjectives
Three verbs (-ing words)
Four words about the subject
Three verbs (-ing words)
Two adjectives
A synonym

Year 8: Diamante Poetry
Annabelle Hogan

THE SEASIDE

Beach
Sunny, hot
Playing, eating, sunbathing,
Sometimes cold, sometimes windy,
Surfing, boating, swimming,
Wet, fun
Sand

AT CHRISTMAS TIME

Christmas
Snowy, cold
Singing, laughing, loving,
Eggnog and hot chocolate
Drinking, eating, talking,
Fireside, stockings
Santa

Year 8: Diamante Poetry
Annabelle Hogan and Bethel Tezera

FAMILY

Family
Caring, loving
Talking, sharing, laughing,
Sometimes annoying, often thoughtful,
Eating, helping, playing,
Funny, thankful
Relatives

EDUCATION

School
Educational, fun
Talking, sharing, laughing
Lots of homework practise
Playing, helping, eating,
Inspiring, helpful
Education

Year 8: Poetry

Etheree

Consists of 10 lines of 1,2,3,4,5,6,7,8,9,10 syllables. Etheree can also be reversed and written 10,9,8,7,6,5,4,3,2,1.

Year 8: Etheree Poetry
Bethel Tezera

SOULJA BOY

Drake
He's nice
Very cool
But very weird
Makes me wonder if
He *is* the best rapper
People say that many times
But I think there's a better one
The rapper for me is Soulja Boy
His catchy music is my favourite.

75

Year 8: Etheree Poetry
Charis Ekanayaka

CHRISTMAS TIME

Elves
Santa
Family
Time for good friends
Building big snowmen
And for advent angels
The best thing at Christmas is
Decorating the Christmas tree,
Singing along to Christmas Carols,
Eating turkey, gravy and fresh carrots.

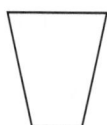

Year 8: Etheree Poetry
Jade Genniges

SPRING IS IN THE AIR

Spring

Frosted

Flowers bloom

Bees buzz around

The sun is shining

The animals wake up

Time to change seasonal wear

"Winter wonderland" has ended

But springtime madness has now begun

All this glory and fun happens in spring.

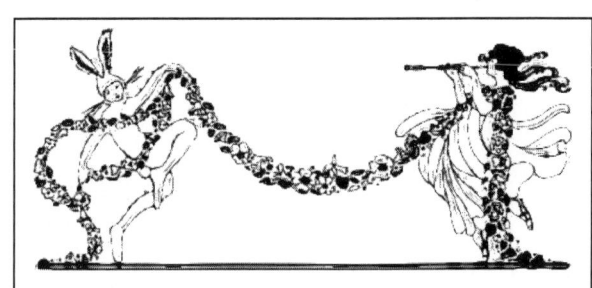

Year 8: Etheree Poetry
Jessica Garcia

WINTER

Snow

It's cold

And it's fun

Making snowmen

Pure as a white dove

We can make snow angels

From soft snow from the sky

I love it when it snows a lot

So we go down big hills on our sleigh

And I wear my warm coat and woolly boots.

Year 8: Etheree Poetry
Rebecca Thomas

PLEASE NOT WORLD WAR THREE

They cover their faces with plastic masks
The men in waiting are coming near
Deathly winds are howling around
Cherry blossoms falling down
The calm before the storm
World war is coming
Darkness is close
Death is here
Despair
War.

Year 9: Articles

Editorials written by the Young Journalists' group using writing prompts from The Metro.

Year 9: Articles using slang and puns

Year 9: Articles using slang and puns
Delia Rainone and Nicole Hidat

Wednesday 21 October 2015

BANG SLANG IN TO THE ROOM
By Nicole Hidat

The baffling way that teenagers talk today can surely spin your head right round. It makes you wonder if they have a different language of their own. Take SNAKE and BAIT... Do you pretend to understand by nodding your head – yes – but wanting to say – no – and just wanting to shout: WHAT DO YOU MEAN?

If you find yourself in that tricky spot, ask yourself: Is it Extraordinary Slanglish or a case of Lost and Sound?

WUU2? ARE ADULTS 'BAFT' ABOUT THIS QUESTION?
By Delia Rainone

Ain't this a slangtastic way to speak? Many adults don't understand the way that teenagers talk. When teens text each other, they use abbreviations for banging convos.

But the differences in the English slanguage are leaving grownups baft. So, what can teenagers do? Spare a thought for parents and let them know "What-you-up-to".

Year 9: Articles on sexism and stereotypes

Year 9: Articles on sexism and stereotypes
Delia Rainone

Wednesday 11 November 2015

All Teenage Girls Judge Other Girls
By Delia Rainone

Some teenage girls can't help but judge a new girl when she comes in and joins her new class, according to a questionnaire done in London schools. They think about whether or not the new girl may be 'different', 'rude' or 'a good person to get along with'.

However, other girls in the class don't appear to care and simply enjoy making new friends and getting along as best they can with the newcomer, rather than judge her on her looks.

One person might stay away from the new classmate because they don't know how she really is, so they don't want her to become a friend, while other girls will go straight up to her and introduce themselves.

Therefore, the next time a new girl joins the class, my advice is: 'don't judge a book by its cover'. Get to know her first and try to have some fun.

Year 9: Articles on sexism and stereotypes
Hyabel Kidane

Wednesday 11 November 2015

The Curse of Teenage Girls
By Hyabel Kidane

Teenage girls are branded as free spirits and as having a lack of responsibility, or are shown as uptight and far smarter than boys in a recent survey.

Opinions ranged from positive to patronising. The stereotype of girls having a simple life and being seen as irresponsible was reinforced by the saying, "Girls just wanna have fun."

However, some girls prove this attitude wrong. Girls like Malala Yousafzai have shown their leadership across the world. A few may even grow to be in charge someday, like Margaret Thatcher.

Year 9: Articles on sexism and stereotypes
Shauna Magee-Foster

Wednesday 11 November 2015

Girl on girl bullying: The stereotyping of teenage girls
By Shauna Magee-Foster

Girls in the world suffer the worst bullying and stereotyping by other girls. But why does this take place and how can we prevent it from happening?

Some girls are told that they lack in responsibility when the truth is they have the responsibility of looking after younger siblings or having to do chores at home.

So the question is: why do girls stereotype other girls?

The problem with some girls is that they don't try understand how other girls have different ways and so they end up bullying each other.

If girls could only learn to get to know their differences, maybe girl bullying wouldn't happen.

Year 9: Articles on fast food and culture

Year 9: Articles on fast food and culture
By Hyabel Kidane and Nicole Hidat

Wednesday 18 November 2015

LOVE AT FIRST SPILL

By Hyabel Kidane and Nicole Hidat

The famous "I'm Lovin' it" advert is apparently true by bringing two people together.

On Tuesday 10 November at the Notting Hill of McDonalds, a man arrived to buy some take away coffee for work. He started to sip his hot drink but spit it out when it burned his mouth. With eyes glaring at him, a cleaner arrived. The man blushed, until she dropped her bucket full of water. All the McDonalds' staff and customers were staring and a few chuckles went around as both man and woman stood in a puddle of water. The man said, "I was in a rush. My boss sent me to get coffee and I made a mistake. When she spilled the bucket, I knew she was just like me."

As they got tissues to clean up the mess of coffee and water, chuckles became cheers and soon the couple were laughing along with the customers and staff. The two people knew it was true love. The woman added, "It was love at first spill."

Year 9: Articles on fast food and culture
Shauna Magee-Foster

Wednesday 18 November 2015

UNHAPPY MAN STEALS HAPPY MEAL

By Shauna Magee-Foster

On Saturday 14 November 2015 at 10:17, a 'stressed' man walked into McDonalds in Hammersmith and waited in line for his order. He rudely demanded a Childrens' Happy meal. The counter lady was confused by his sudden outburst, but got his meal and gave it to him. He looked once towards the door and quickly ran off without paying. As he escaped, he threw his wrapper on the floor and swore at shocked customers, who didn't do anything to stop him. The man rushed towards the bus stop and got on a bus, again without paying.

If anyone has any information, please contact the local police station.

Year 9: Articles interpreting newspaper headlines

Year 9: Articles interpreting newspaper headlines
Delia Rainone

Wednesday 21 November 2015

READ THE FINE PRINT...£60 FOR DROPPING A BOOKMARK

By Delia Rainone

On Saturday 17 November at 2.45pm, a beagle dog entered a shop through the automatic doors and took a bookmark. The customers and shop workers realised what had happened when they heard the beeping sound of something getting stolen.

The shop manager chased the small dog up to Hyde Park and found him leading his way to a man sitting on a bench. The dog dropped the bookmark right in front of his owner.

The beagle owner got fined £60 and was accused of making the dog steal the bookmark deliberately. The man was acting suspiciously and said repeatedly, "Why are you blaming me? My dog doesn't know anything. He probably wandered off while I was on my phone and saw a nice bookmark to play with." The man kept acting suspiciously and even though he claimed he didn't train the dog to steal it, he put the stolen bookmark in his book when questioned.

Year 9: Articles interpreting newspaper headlines
Hyabel Kidane

Wednesday 21 November 2015

READ THE FINE PRINT...£60 FOR DROPPING A BOOKMARK
By Hyabel Kidane

You would expect a big time celebrity darling to maybe get a bit carried away on a shopping trip. But not for Paul McCartney.

On Wednesday 21 November, he was having a quiet day book shopping in London. But what he didn't know was that he would be in more trouble than getting carried away on a night out.

As he was buying his book, he dropped a bookmark and accidently stepped on it, ripping it. He gave a little chuckle and said, "Sorry." But the shopkeeper was in no mood to laugh. "He shouted and screamed and at first I thought he was joking," said the confused Paul McCartney.

But there was no happy ending. Nobody was singing 'Help!' for him after being fined £60.

Year 9: Articles interpreting newspaper headlines
Shauna Magee-Foster

Wednesday 21 November 2015

READ THE FINE PRINT...£60 FOR DROPPING A BOOKMARK

By Shauna Magee-Foster

On Monday 19 November 2015, a London secondary school teacher was fined £60 by the Headteacher for littering.

The teacher from Gunners School, London threw a bookmark to a student because she kept losing her place. However, she didn't catch it because the teacher didn't aim towards her and the bookmark dropped on the floor. The teacher was then fined for littering.

The student said, "Mr McDonald was bent when he threw a bookmark to me and I can't believe that he got fined for that."

Mr McDonald and the Headteacher were not available for comment.

#0108 - 030516 - C0 - 210/148/5 - PB - DID1442756